OCEAN FRIENDS

This book belongs to:

_____

OCEAN FRIENDS

by Robert Lyn Nelson

NorthWord Press
Chanhassen, Minnesota

The text and display type were set in Caslon, Khaki, and Mini Pics Lil Fishies
Composed in the United States of America
Designed by Lois A. Rainwater
Edited by Aimee Jackson

Books for Young Readers
NorthWord Press
18705 Lake Drive East
Chanhassen, MN 55317
www.northwordpress.com

Library of Congress Cataloging-in-Publication Data

Nelson, Robert Lyn, 1955-
Ocean friends / by Robert Lyn Nelson
p. cm.
Summary: Describes the ocean world of Naia, a bottlenose dolphin, and the other marine animals around her.
ISBN 1-55971-840-4 (hc.)
1. Marine animals—Juvenile literature. [1. Bottlenose dolphin. 2. Dolphins. 3. Marine animals. 4. Ocean.] I. Title.

QL122.2.N44 2002

591.77—dc21

2002032641

Nelson

Printed in Singapore
10 9 8 7 6 5 4 3 2 1

For Margaux and Sienna

—R. L. N.

This is Naia. She is a bottlenose dolphin. Naia lives in the beautiful blue sea, but she is not a fish. She swims all day, but she is a mammal and breathes air just as people do.

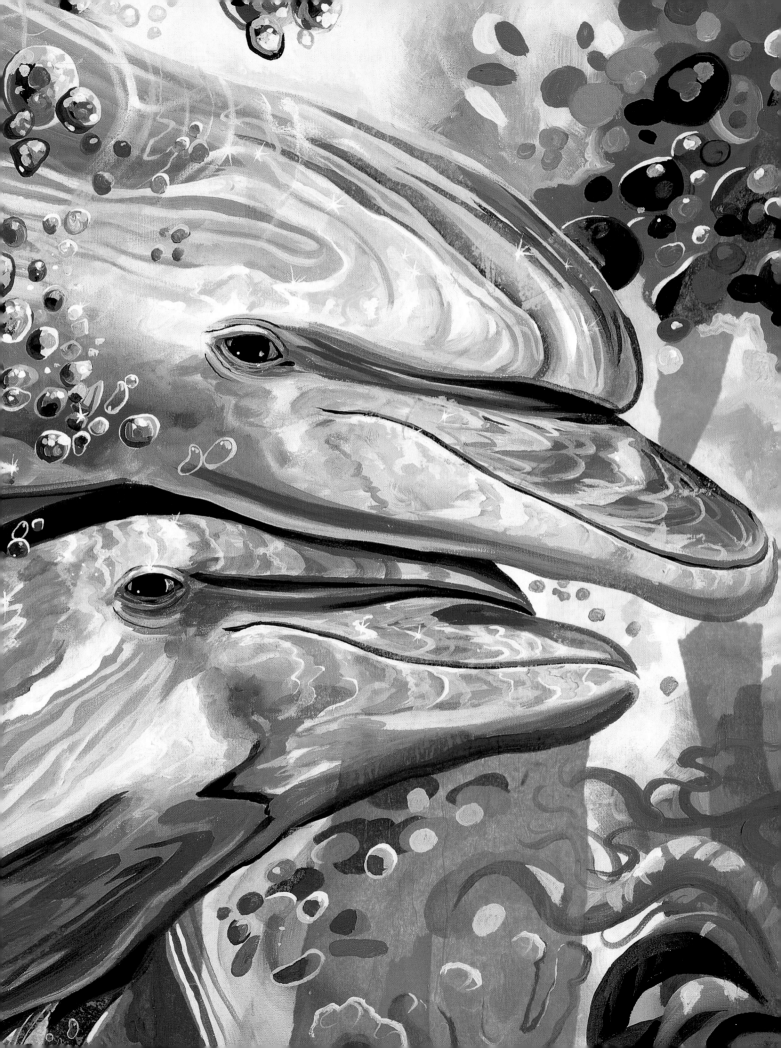

Dolphin bodies are sleek and smooth. They can swim through the water as fast as some birds can fly through the sky. Below the waves, they fly over coral reefs that shine like rainbows.

Rain falls on the mountains and creates streams that flow into the sea. In her ocean home, Naia swims through water that fell from the sky and traveled across the land. Water is precious to all the creatures of the earth.

The ocean is filled with color.
In the warm waters, tropical fish
look like they were painted by
an artist! The sun from the world
above shines through the water
with a sparkling light.

Sometimes in her ocean home,
Naia sees strange things from the
world above. There are sunken
ships that no longer ride the waves.
Now these ships lie peacefully
among the sea fans and sponges.

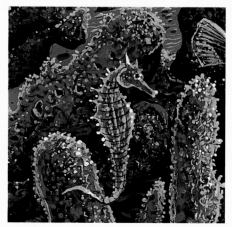

Long ago
there were
people who
lived in great
stone cities.
Now some
of these cities
are part of
the mystery
of this ocean
home. Deep
in the sea,
Naia visits
her friends
the sea turtles.
Together
they swim
among the
silent towers.

Naia has many wonderful friends in her ocean home. There are playful sea otters and seals, brightly colored fish, gentle whales, and fascinating squids and rays.

Naia's friend the manta ray
is one of the most graceful
creatures in the sea. With giant
wings, he swoops through the
sparkling water.

There are many types of whales in the ocean. These black and white hunters are Naia's cousins, the orca whales.

The gray whales are Naia's friends,
too. The little calves swim close to
their mothers where they are safe.
Although gray whales are very
large creatures, they are very gentle.

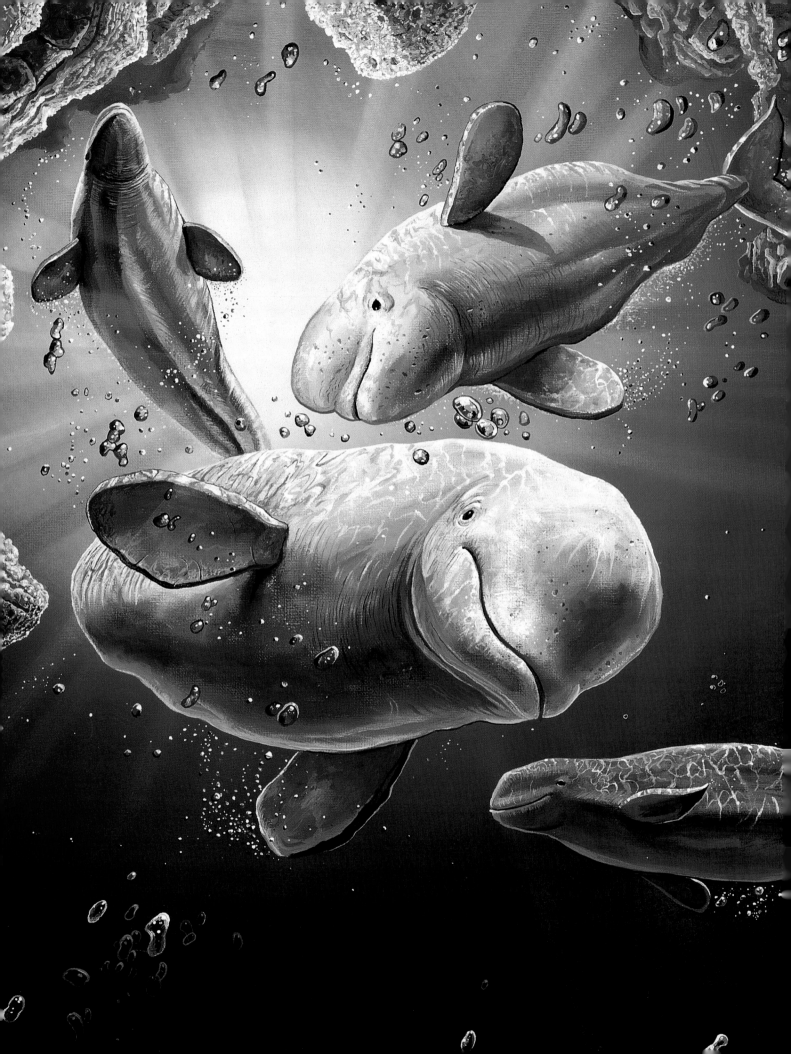

In the polar waters, ice floats
above. The sea is cold, but
it is a perfect home for the
beluga whales.

Naia has many
wonderful friends
in her ocean home.

As
twilight
ends,
the
silhouette
of a new
island
appears.

Some day there will be mountains and forests on this island. Rain will fall on these mountains, and new streams will flow into the sea.

ROBERT LYN NELSON has traveled the world researching and gathering pictures for his books. He is a dedicated conservationist, striving to build interest and concern for animals and nature through his art and words. Nelson has donated his time and work to several environmental organizations, including the National Geographic Society, the World Wildlife Federation, and the National Marine Sanctuary Program. He has earned international acclaim and awards, including being named "Environmental Hero" by the White House. Robert Lyn Nelson lives in Hawaii.